Copyright © 1998 by Nord-Süd Verlag AG, Gossau Zürich, Switzerland.
First published in Switzerland under the title *Leb wohl, Chaja!*
English translation copyright © 1998 by North-South Books Inc.

All rights reserved.
No part of this book may be reproduced or utilized in any form
or by any means, electronic or mechanical, including photocopying,
recording, or any information storage and retrieval system,
without permission in writing from the publisher.

First published in the United States, Great Britain, Canada,
Australia, and New Zealand in 1998 by North-South Books,
an imprint of Nord-Süd Verlag AG, Gossau Zürich, Switzerland.

Distributed in the United States by North-South Books Inc., New York.

Library of Congress Cataloging-in-Publication Data is available.
A CIP catalogue record for this book is available from The British Library.
ISBN 1-55858-985-6 (trade binding)
1 3 5 7 9 TB 10 8 6 4 2
ISBN 1-55858-986-4 (library binding)
1 3 5 7 9 LB 10 8 6 4 2
Printed in Belgium

For more information about our books, and the authors and artists
who create them, visit our web site: http://www.northsouth.com

Antonie Schneider

Good-Bye, Vivi!

Illustrated by Maja Dusíková

Translated by J. Alison James

North-South Books · New York · London

On the day Granny came with her big umbrella to live with
Molly and Will, the sun was shining. She got out of Papa's car
carrying a box poked full of little holes. "I brought Vivi with
me," she said. "I couldn't bear to leave her behind."

"Vivi?" asked Molly.

"You remember, my canary. She keeps me feeling lively,
like her name."

There was a good sunny place for Vivi on the kitchen windowsill. Granny set up her cage with a bowl for food and a little bathhouse. Vivi was delighted. Granny sat down next to the cage and whistled a song. Vivi cocked her little head and listened.

That's how it all began, Vivi and Granny, Mama and Papa, Molly and her little brother Will, all living together in the same big house. Soon they grew accustomed to the new arrangement. Even Papa stopped being annoyed by Vivi's fluttering and peeping in the mornings.

Every afternoon Molly gave her a piece of apple.

"Let Vivi fly free around the kitchen," Granny said, "or her wings will get rusty."

When Will brought her a dandelion petal, she splashed in the birdbath.

Granny often sat near Vivi at the window. They liked to listen to the radio. Granny loved opera best of all, and Vivi would sing along. Whenever Molly and Will fought, Vivi cheeped excitedly. That made them laugh and they would forget their fight.

That autumn, Vivi lost more feathers than usual.

"It's what happens," Mama said. "Vivi is growing her winter clothes."

Granny began to complain of being tired. When she went on her Sunday walk with Papa, she leaned on her big umbrella. She slept more than before. She also couldn't hear as well. And when she got letters, she read them almost as slowly as Will did. Often she pulled photos out and told Molly stories about Vivi, like the time she washed the dishes, or spilled coffee with her tail.

The snow came. Granny seldom left the house now. She sat near Vivi at the window.

On a cold January morning, when Molly and Will came into the kitchen, Vivi was not on her perch. She sat on the bottom of the cage with her eyes half closed.

"What's wrong?" asked Will, worried. "Vivi won't eat anything. She won't even take a bath."

"Vivi's old, for a bird," said Granny. "Perhaps she's tired. Her old body is probably full of aches and pains."

So Molly made the little bird a soft nest of lamb's wool and cotton. Will held her in his arms to keep her warm.

"Vivi looks content that way," said Granny.

Outside the snow fell in deep drifts.

Mama dripped water into Vivi's beak. Suddenly Vivi fluttered wildly, and Will was startled. But he stroked her feathers smooth, and she nestled down into his arms again.

That night Molly and Will put Vivi to bed in her little nest on the floor of the cage. Mama laid a tea towel over the top so Vivi would be shaded from the light.

Early in the morning, Will ran into the kitchen. He looked at Vivi. She was still sleeping. Will stood there a long time, waiting for the bird to wake up. Outside the window, snow fell thickly. Vivi was so still, she wasn't even breathing.

Molly came in and stood beside Will.

"Vivi died," he said.

Molly nodded and hugged her little brother.

They both cried.

When Granny got up, she laid her best embroidered handkerchief over Vivi's body.

Papa dug a deep hole in the snow under the spruce tree in the garden. Even Granny came out, holding Mama's arm.

Will laid Vivi tenderly in the hole, and Papa covered her over.

"You pretty golden bird," said Molly softly.

Granny started to sing a song, and they all joined in.

It was so quiet back in the kitchen. Mother had put the cage out in the shed. Now Granny sat alone at the window.

Will looked out at the spruce tree where Vivi was buried. "Granny?" asked Will. "Will you die someday?"

Granny nodded. "I am old and tired just like Vivi," she said. "When my time comes, I'll die too. But you remember all kinds of things about Vivi, don't you? Vivi lives in our memories. In the same way I'll always be with you. You can keep your memories alive by telling stories and looking at pictures." She pulled out a picture of Vivi. "Here, look at this."

Will climbed up on her lap. "That is Vivi!" he said.

"I'll give it to you," said Granny, and then she told him a story about Vivi.

A sunbeam fell on Vivi's place on the windowsill. When
Will saw it, he remembered Vivi's chirping.

"Will you come with me to visit Vivi's grave?" asked Will.

It took Granny a little while to get her coat on and find her
umbrella.

Will carefully took her hand and held it tightly as they
walked across the snow.

Granny brought a ring of birdseed in the pocket of her
coat. She tied it onto a spruce bough just over Vivi's grave.
Then she went back into the house. Granny went heavily
up the stairs.

That spring Granny didn't sit so often at the window. She preferred to lie on the sofa or sit in her warm bed. Once she said, "You two won't ever leave me alone, will you?"

"Never, Granny, never!" cried Will, shocked.

Then Granny stretched out her arms and gave Molly and Will a kiss. "Good, good," she said, contented.

Molly and Will liked to play games with Granny after school.
Sometimes she told them stories of when she was a little girl.
Sometimes she told them Vivi stories. Will realized she'd been
right. After all this time, he still remembered Vivi.

One morning Mama woke the children. She'd been crying.
Behind her stood Papa.

"Granny died in the night," said Mama, and she took Molly
and Will by the hand. Granny lay quite still, more still and more
quiet than when she was sleeping.

"Granny!" Will shouted, but she still did not move. "Granny,
wake up!" He held her hand, but she did not hold his hand back.
Granny wasn't there anymore.

Mama and Papa, Molly and Will stood by Granny's bedside
and cried. Outside the birds were singing. The birds couldn't
understand how they felt.

Later that day Mama came into the children's room.

"Do you remember," she asked, "how Granny said that people live on in your memories?"

Molly and Will nodded.

"I found this among her things." It was a book, full of pictures and stories.

Molly opened it and read it aloud to Will:

Stories from My Vivi (Vivi means Life!)
for Molly and Will

"I remember you, Granny," said Will.

"And we'll read your stories," added Molly, "and tell them to each other so we'll never forget."

Tea time

Will learns to whistle.

Vivi takes a ribbon 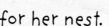 for her nest.

Crash landing!

Vivi washes the dishes.

Vivi sings an aria from the opera—soprano part.

When Vivi sleeps,
no bells can wake her.

Vivi does Molly's hair.

Vivi makes new friends.